For all Owls: Big, Small or Eggs.
This one's for you with love – DG

For Edward and Isobel – AB

Bloomsbury Publishing, London, Oxford, New York, New Delhi and Sydney

First published in Great Britain in 2016 by Bloomsbury Publishing Plc
50 Bedford Square, London, WC1B 3DP

www.bloomsbury.com

BLOOMSBURY is a registered trademark of Bloomsbury Publishing Plc

Text copyright © Debi Gliori 2016
Illustration copyright © Alison Brown 2016
The moral rights of the author and illustrator have been asserted

A CIP catalogue record of this book is available from the British Library

ISBN 978 1 4088 5378 8 (HB)
ISBN 978 1 4088 5379 5 (PB)
ISBN 978 1 4088 5380 1 (eBook)

All papers used by Bloomsbury Publishing are natural, recyclable products made from
wood grown in well managed forests. The manufacturing processes conform to
the environmental regulations of the country of origin

Printed in China by Leo Paper Products, Heshan, Guangdong

1 3 5 7 9 10 8 6 4 2

Little Owl's Egg

Debi Gliori   Alison Brown

BLOOMSBURY

LONDON OXFORD NEW YORK NEW DELHI SYDNEY

Little Owl's mummy had some
very exciting news.
She had laid a beautiful egg.

"Guess what?" said Little Owl's mummy.
"We're having a new baby owl."

"NO," said Little Owl.

"NO,

NO,

NO!"

"No?" said Mummy.

"NO," said Little Owl.
"I'm your baby owl. You
don't need a new one."

Mummy Owl blinked.
"Silly me," she said. "You're right.
Besides, this egg is far too quiet
to be a baby owl . . .

. . . perhaps it's a baby worm.
They're so silent and undemanding.
Just a bowl of earth from time
to time . . . Wouldn't that be lovely?"

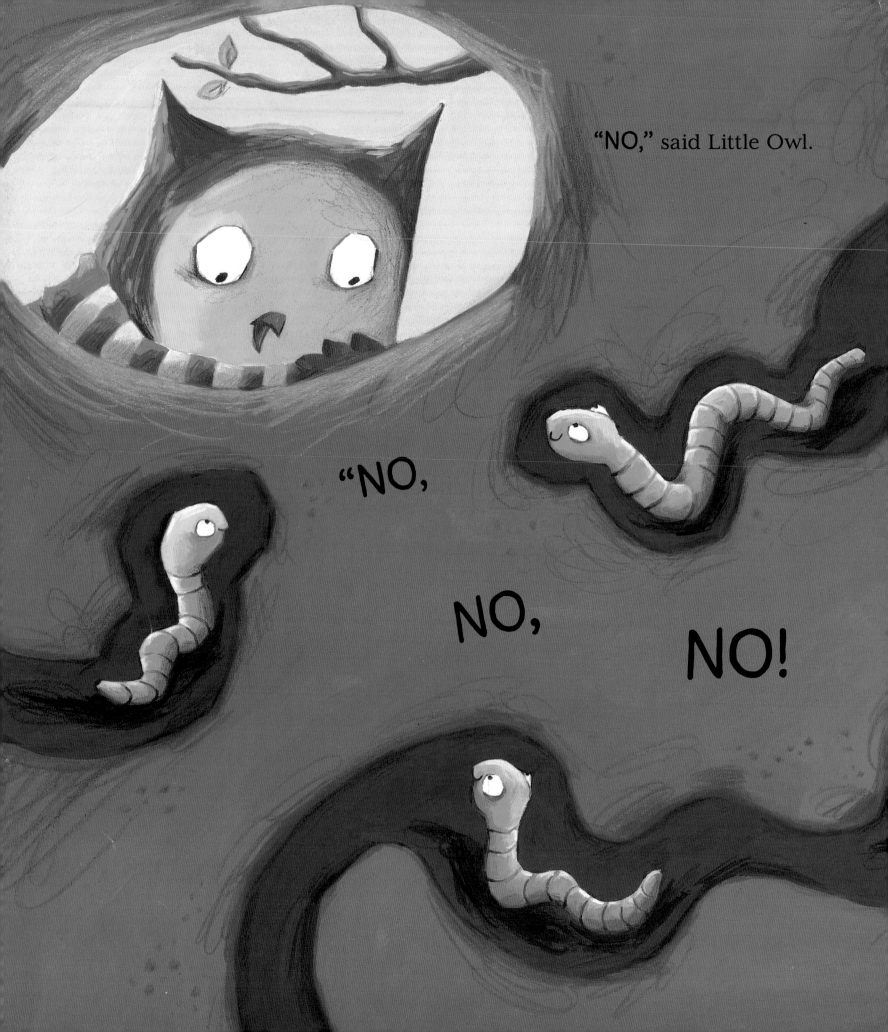

"NO," said Little Owl.

"NO, NO, NO!

Not a wiggly worm.

EWWWWW."

Mummy Owl smiled.

"No," she said. "You're right.

It doesn't **wiggle**.

Perhaps it's a pretend egg.

Made of **chocolate** . . .

. . . wouldn't **that** be good?"

"**No**," sighed Little Owl.

"**Chocolate** eggs are no fun.

They don't know how to play.

And they melt if you hug them."

Mummy Owl prodded the egg.
"You're right, Little Owl. This egg is
far too cold to be made of chocolate.
Poor egg. Feel it – it's freezing.

I wonder if we're having
a baby penguin. Heavens.
We'd better go and catch
some fish for its dinner."

penguin. Fish? YUCK!"

Mummy Owl patted the egg. "What a
silly mummy – penguin eggs are warm.
It's crocodile eggs that are chilly.
That's it. We're having a baby crocodile.
I wonder what they eat?"

Little Owl's eyes grew **wide**.

"N-n-n-no," he whispered, "n-n-not a crocodile."

"Probably not," whispered Mummy.
"Besides, it's a **huge egg**. Far too
big to be a crocodile.
Perhaps it's an . . ."

"ELEPHANT!" yelled Little Owl.
"That would be amazing. We could have
the best water fights . . ."

"No," said Mummy.
"NO, NO, NO! Think
of our nest. That would
be a catastrophe."

"No. You're right," said Little Owl.
"Besides, **elephants** can't fly.
But **dragons** can. Ooooh.
I hope it's a **dragon egg**."

"HEAVEN FORBID,"
squeaked Mummy.
"NO, NO, NO!"

"But it is a very splendid
egg," said Little Owl.
"It must have something
very **special** inside . . .

Perhaps it's a baby

Princess Wormy Choco-Penguin Crocophant Dragowl.

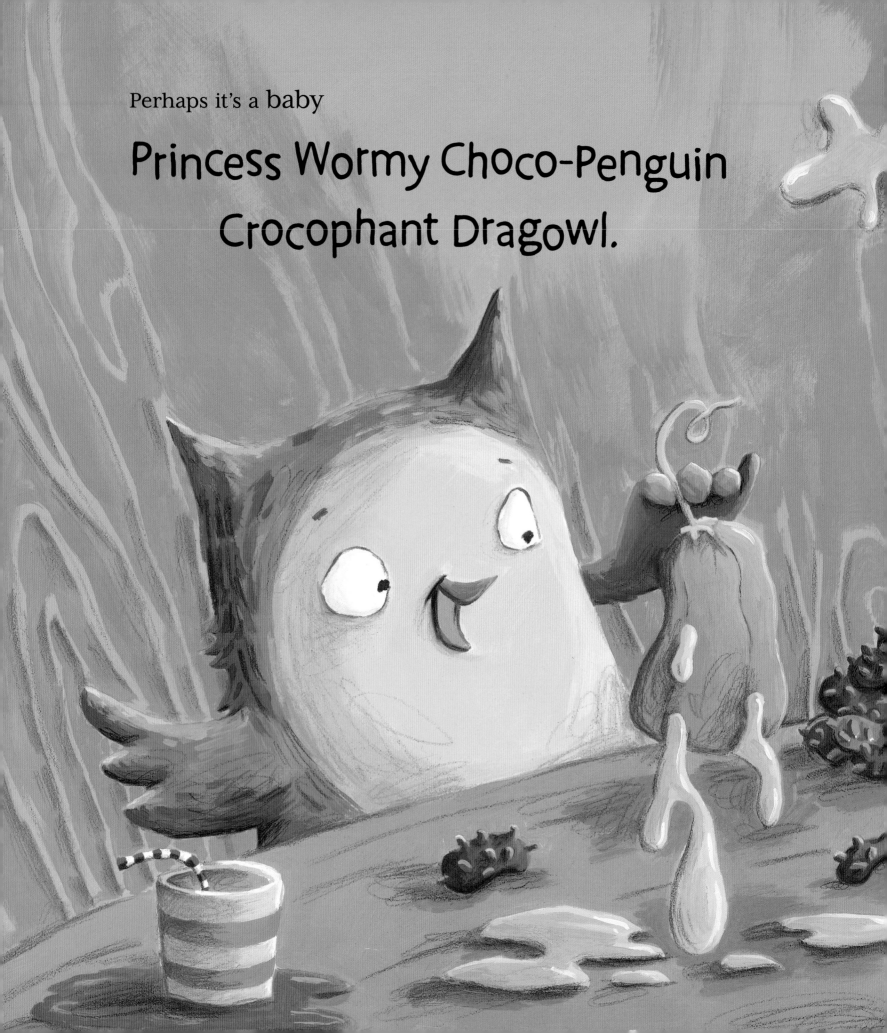

Hmmm. I've heard that they only eat very special food. Eighty-legged snort beans. Green-gloopy gargle tubers . . ."

"Sounds awful,"
groaned Mummy.

"D'you know," continued Little Owl, "a little owl just like me would be much more fun than a baby Princess Wormy Choco-Penguin Crocophant Dragowl."

"Yes," said Mummy. "We'd love a baby owl much more than a baby anything else."

Little Owl put his wings round the egg and gave
it a hug. Inside, a tiny heart beat steadily.

Thud

Thud

Thud

"When will our egg be ready?" said Little Owl.

"Soon," said Mummy.

"If it's a new Little Owl, then I'll be
a new Big Owl," said Little Owl.

"Yes," said Mummy. "You'll be my new
Big Owl, and I'll love you always."

"Always?"
said Little Owl.

"Always," said Mummy.